MY GRANDPA'S CHAIR

by Jiyeon Pak

ALFRED A. KNOPF NEW YORK

My grandpa used to love reading
on his old couch.

But lately, he didn't seem
happy when he sat there.

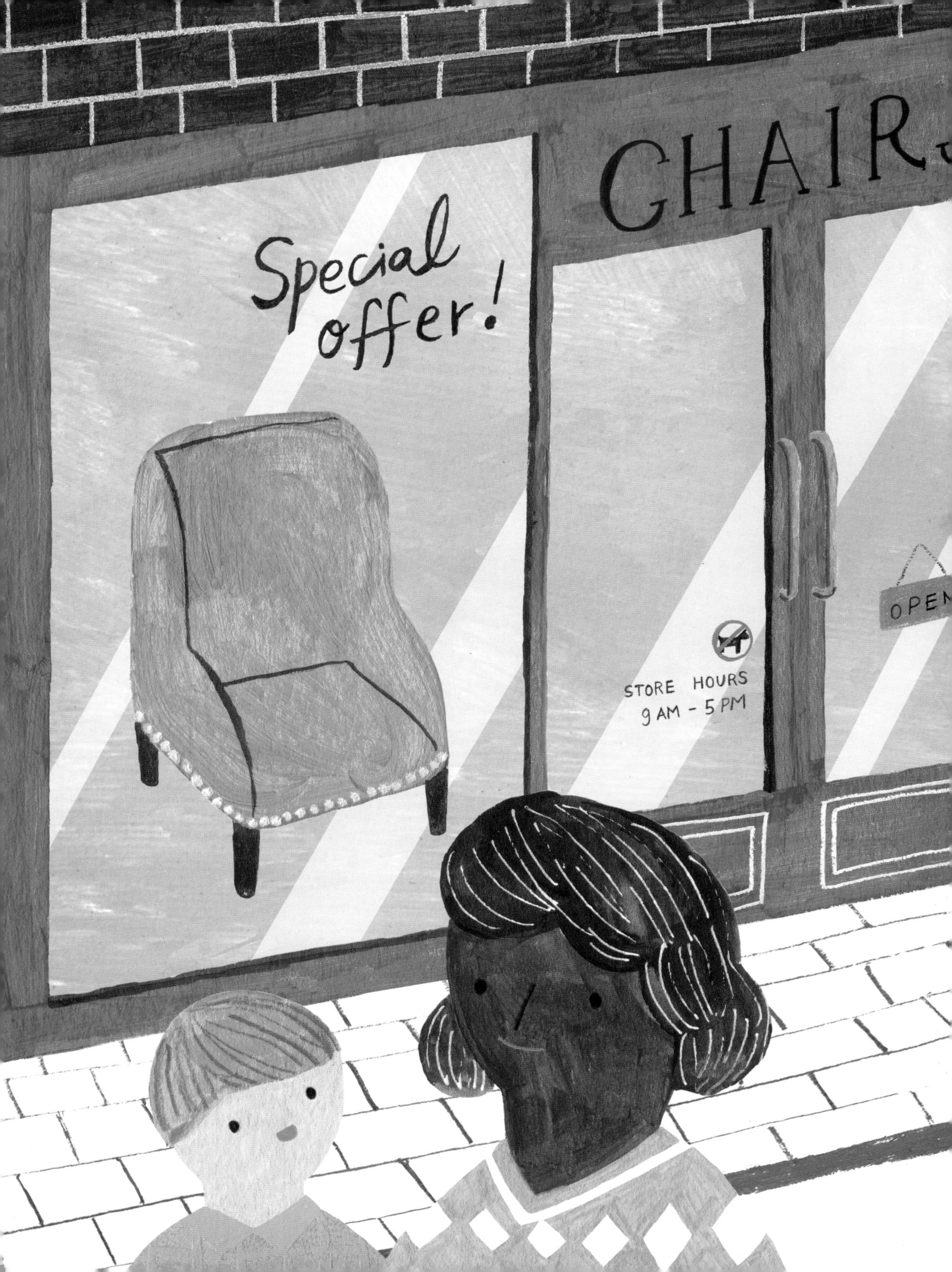

Special offer!
STORE HOURS
9 AM - 5 PM

I thought Grandpa might need a new chair, so Mimi and I took him shopping.

The store had all sorts of chairs.

Some chairs were too small.

The hard chair gave him back pain.

The rocking chair
made Grandpa dizzy.

And some chairs
were too soft.

None of the store chairs were quite right. Grandpa decided to order a chair that was made just for him.

A famous craftsman
cut down the tree,

carved the wood, and
assembled the parts.

It was one of a kind,
made especially for
my grandpa.

But the new chair made
Grandpa worry.

What if Mimi
scratched it?

What if he spilled
his tea on it?

Eventually, Grandpa put the chair in a room where nothing would damage it.

Mimi and I decided to take Grandpa
to our favorite place to cheer him up.

18
19
20

30

The park was filled with
people enjoying the
fresh air and sunshine.

Mimi and I chased ducks. We said hello to a squirrel and smelled flowers.

After a while, I needed to sit down. Grandpa came with me.

Lucy

And guess what?
Grandpa finally found a seat
that made him happy.

For the ones who believe in me and my dream

THIS IS A BORZOI BOOK PUBLISHED BY ALFRED A. KNOPF

 Published in the United States by Alfred A. Knopf,
an imprint of Random House Children's Books, a division of Penguin Random House LLC, New York.

Knopf, Borzoi Books, and the colophon are registered trademarks of Penguin Random House LLC.

Visit us on the Web! randomhousekids.com

Educators and librarians, for a variety of teaching tools, visit us at RHTeachersLibrarians.com

Library of Congress Cataloging-in-Publication data is available upon request.
ISBN 978-1-5247-0075-1 (hardcover) — ISBN 978-1-5247-0076-8 (lib. bdg.) —
ISBN 978-1-5247-0077-5 (ebook)

MANUFACTURED IN CHINA

September 2017

10 9 8 7 6 5 4 3 2 1

First Edition

Random House Children's Books supports the First Amendment and celebrates the right to read.